AARDMAN
CHICKEN RUN
DAWN OF THE NUGGET

Macmillan Children's Books

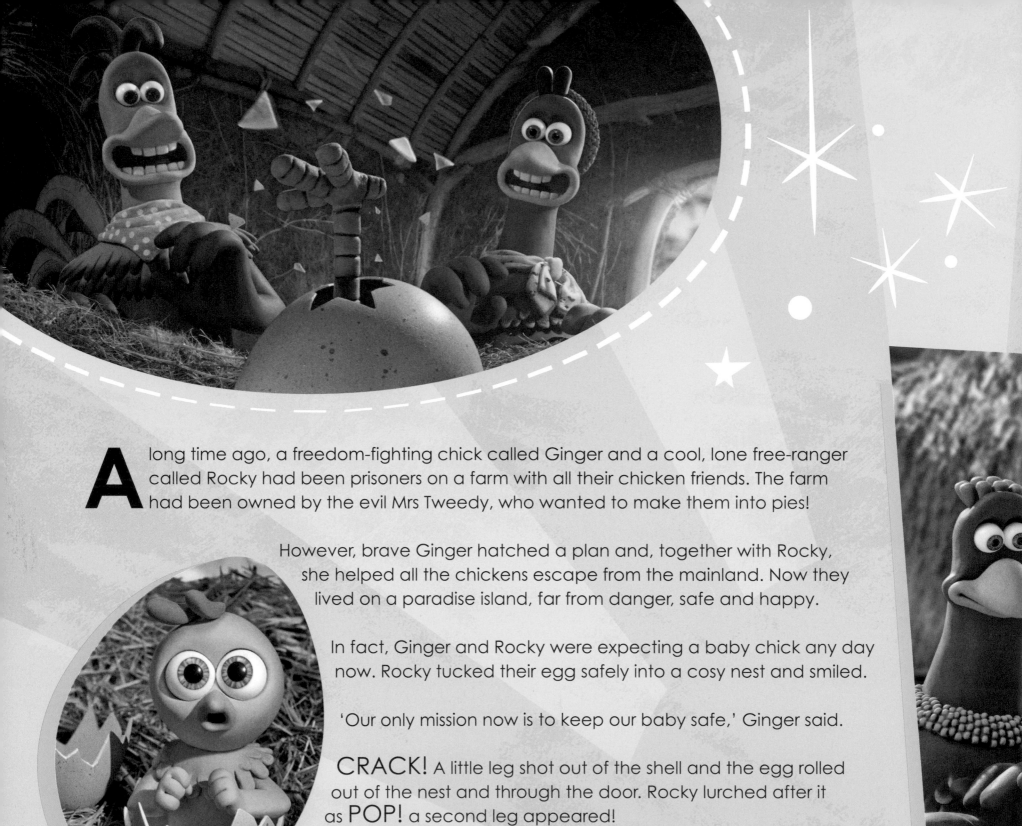

A long time ago, a freedom-fighting chick called Ginger and a cool, lone free-ranger called Rocky had been prisoners on a farm with all their chicken friends. The farm had been owned by the evil Mrs Tweedy, who wanted to make them into pies!

However, brave Ginger hatched a plan and, together with Rocky, she helped all the chickens escape from the mainland. Now they lived on a paradise island, far from danger, safe and happy.

In fact, Ginger and Rocky were expecting a baby chick any day now. Rocky tucked their egg safely into a cosy nest and smiled.

'Our only mission now is to keep our baby safe,' Ginger said.

CRACK! A little leg shot out of the shell and the egg rolled out of the nest and through the door. Rocky lurched after it as POP! a second leg appeared!

'Grab it!' Ginger cried.

But too late – the egg launched itself through the air, giggling, before landing with a THUMP in a pile of hay. Ginger and Rocky ran over to hug their new chick.

'She's perfect!' said Ginger. 'Welcome to the world – Molly!'

Molly grew up curious, constantly looking for adventure – and she didn't always follow the rules . . . One day, she even slipped onto a raft with her favourite uncles – the rats, Nick and Fetcher – and sailed away! Luckily, Rocky spotted her just in time and brought her home.

Molly longed to explore the mainland. But when she asked her parents about it, Rocky would distract her with one of his favourite tricks: making popcorn. Ginger didn't want Molly to know about their past lives. She just wanted to keep Molly safe on the island.

One day, Ginger spotted a **Fun-Land Farms** truck driving along a new road on the mainland. The sound of chickens clucking carried across the water and her stomach dropped. She called an emergency meeting.

'A chicken farm!' cried the frightened birds. 'What if the humans find us?'

Ginger nodded. 'We have to hide,' she said. 'We'll build a giant screen of leaves around the island.'

Bunty and Mac were very surprised. Hide? This wasn't the brave Ginger they knew!

'I have Molly to think about now,' said Ginger. 'I can't put her in danger!'

The next day, Molly saw the truck too. 'What is that?' she asked. 'I want to go and see it!'

'No, Molly,' said Ginger. 'You've got everything you need here on the island.'

'Except for my freedom!' cried Molly, storming off. Why did her mother always treat her like a baby?

That night, Ginger dreamt that Molly was in danger. She woke in a panic and rushed into Molly's room. Her bed was empty!

'Molly's left the island!' cried Ginger, waking Rocky. 'We have to find her!'

Molly had taken a raft to the mainland and was standing on a dark road. WHOOSH! A big Fun-Land truck came along – and a chicken pushed Molly out of the way just in time.

'Woah!' said the chicken. 'Isn't it a bit late for you to be out, baby girl?'

'I'm not a baby girl!' said Molly, crossly. 'And isn't it late for you to be out, too?'

The chicken laughed. 'You give as good as you get! I'm Frizzle.' She held out her hand.

Frizzle explained how a Fun-Land truck had picked up chickens from her farm, but she was too small to go with them. Now she was following them.

'Fun-Land Farms will be the adventure of a lifetime!' said Frizzle, excitedly. Molly grinned.

The Fun-Land truck had stopped at a petrol station nearby. This was their chance!

'Come on,' Frizzle said, grabbing Molly's hand and running to the truck. 'It's me and you, kidda – all the way!'

Meanwhile, Ginger and Rocky had canoed to the mainland with Babs, Bunty, Mac and Fowler. As they emerged from the trees onto a big road, they saw a driver putting Molly and Frizzle in a truck!

'Molly!' screamed Ginger, but the truck drove off. Thinking fast, Rocky and Ginger jumped onto the back while the others whizzed behind on a trolley. When the truck turned into the farm entrance, they were all flung off and into a hedge.

'That doesn't look so bad!' said Rocky, seeing a sign for the farm. Then he noticed the huge grey building like a prison behind it, surrounded by a moat. This was the REAL Fun-Land Farms!

'That looks SO bad!' said a shocked Rocky.

Inside Fun-Land Farms, Molly and Frizzle were dumped onto a conveyor belt with the other chickens. A robot arm was putting collars around the chickens' necks. Molly and Frizzle didn't like the look of that, so they jumped off the conveyor belt, slid down a chute . . .

. . . and landed in the best place Molly had ever seen! There were egg-cup rides, swimming pools – even an all-you-can-eat buffet!

'Did I promise you the adventure of a lifetime or what!' said Frizzle, in delight. 'Let's play!'

Outside, Rocky and the gang were staring in horror at Fun-Land Farms.

'I've got a plan,' Rocky said. 'I'm gonna go in . . . and bust Molly out of there!'

Before Ginger could say another word, Fowler tied Rocky to a small tree, bent it backwards and let it go.

'FIRE!'

Rocky shot upwards – and got caught on the electric fence. BZZZZ! He fell to the ground in a heap. BANG, BANG! Mechanical moles popped out of the ground and started shooting at him. Rocky ran for the moat as fast as hc could – where he was met by a small army of robot ducks with laser eyes. BOOM! A huge explosion launched him into the air and over the wall into Fun-Land Farms. Rocky was inside!

Having seen all the ways NOT to break in, Ginger and the others hatched a plan with Nick and Fetcher, who lived in a junkyard nearby, and made their move. Quick as a flash, they surprised the guard, snuck under the electric fence, scuba dived through the moat and got past the electronic eye scanner. Easy!

Meanwhile, Fowler, Nick and Fetcher flew in on a cloud balloon and landed on the roof. The rats left Fowler to plan the getaway, and scurried into an air vent. They were in!

Fun-Land was great but Molly soon noticed
that all the chickens looked odd and
a bit . . . brainless.

'There's something strange about this place,'
she said.

'Hmm,' said Frizzle, looking at a grassy mound.
It was propped up by wooden scaffolding.
'It's fake!' she said. They looked closer.
Everything in Fun-Land was fake, even the sky!

Hidden above, a
spy camera turned
towards Frizzle. She
was being watched.
By a man in a secret
control room . . .

'Why haven't you got a collar?' said the man. His name was Dr Fry. Putting on a chicken suit, he entered Fun-Land through a trapdoor. Molly hid just in time and watched in horror as Dr Fry snapped a collar around Frizzle's neck and walked away.

As soon as the collar clicked into place, Frizzle's face went blank, just like the other chickens.

'Who are you?' she said to Molly. Molly's heart sank. Why didn't her friend recognise her?

'I'm going to find out what's going on here, Frizzle,' she said. 'I'll be back. I promise!'

Molly followed Dr Fry out of Fun-Land to a reception area, where a man was waiting. This was Mr Smith, owner of the chain of 'Sir Eat-A-Lot' restaurants.

'Welcome!' said Dr Fry. 'Please follow me to our presentation.'

Ginger had led the gang into the reception area by hiding behind some cleaning supplies. They arrived just in time to see Molly following the two men through a security door.

'Molly!' cried Ginger. She ran and slid through the door before it closed, but the others got left behind.

Molly followed the men to a control room, with Ginger close behind. Dr Fry hit a switch and a chicken appeared on a screen.

'This is a chicken,' said a voice. 'It experiences fear and panic when faced with processing.'

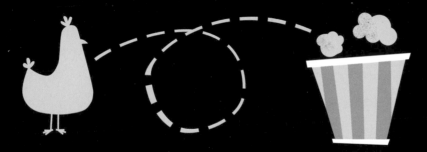

The voice explained that the meat from this chicken was tough and dry. But what if the chicken wasn't scared?

'A happy chicken is a tasty chicken!' it said. A bucket of chicken nuggets appeared.

Molly gasped. Fun-Land made chickens happy – happy to be made into *nuggets!*

'Very clever, Dr Fry!' said Mr Smith. 'But can you do it?'

'We already have!' boomed a voice. A terrifying person appeared. It was – MRS TWEEDY!

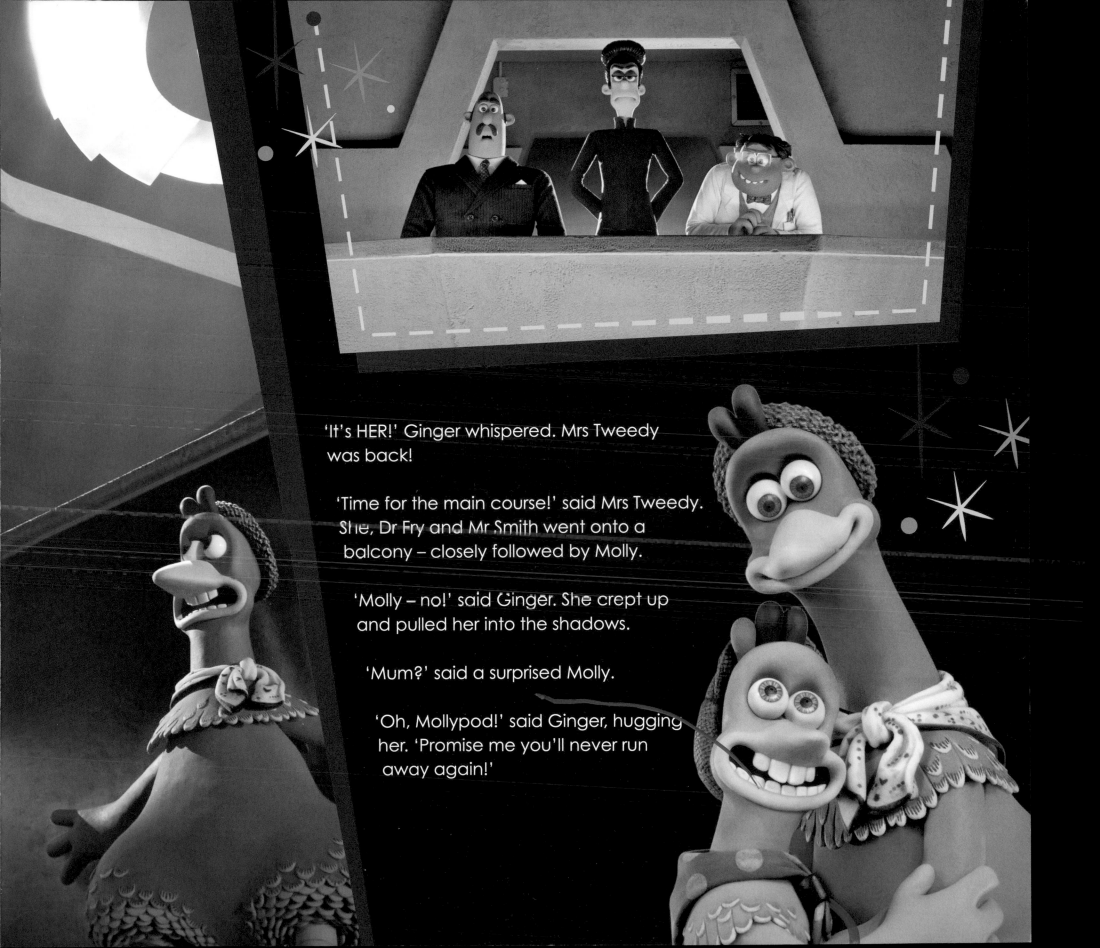

'It's HER!' Ginger whispered. Mrs Tweedy was back!

'Time for the main course!' said Mrs Tweedy. She, Dr Fry and Mr Smith went onto a balcony – closely followed by Molly.

'Molly – no!' said Ginger. She crept up and pulled her into the shadows.

'Mum?' said a surprised Molly.

'Oh, Mollypod!' said Ginger, hugging her. 'Promise me you'll never run away again!'

Dr Fry pressed a number on a remote control. Below them, Chicken 314's collar began to flash.

'I"ve won the prize!' cried the excited chicken. A fake hill slid open to reveal a moving escalator. Chicken 314 went up it, disappearing at the top.

'No!' said Ginger. 'Molly – don't look!'

There was a loud noise, and then a bucket of hot chicken nuggets shot out of a hatch.

'Behold!' announced Mrs Tweedy. **'THE DAWN OF THE NUGGET!'**

Mr Smith grabbed a nugget from the bucket and took a bite. He smacked his lips. 'I'll send a truck for the first batch!' he said.

'Let's get out of here,' said Ginger, in a panic, pulling Molly along.

'Not without Frizzle,' said Molly. 'She's my FRIEND. I can't leave her here!'

'Molly, listen!' Ginger shouted. 'You don't know what you're dealing with!'

'YOU!' cried Mrs Tweedy, spotting Ginger. Ginger ran – but Mrs Tweedy grabbed her.

'You won't ruin my plan again!' she cried. 'Bring me a collar, Dr Fry!'

Elsewhere in the compound, Nick and Fetcher had found Rocky in the air vents . . . and quickly got lost. Suddenly Rocky heard a voice he thought he recognised.

'Here's the miserable chicken that escaped Tweedy's Chicken Farm and ruined my life!'

He looked through a grate to see Ginger – a prisoner of MRS TWEEDY!

'I've got to get in there!' cried Rocky. Nick pointed to an old fan in the vent.

'You used to get shot out of a cannon, right?' he said. 'Fetcher can get this working again.'

For the second time that day, Rocky was launched!

As Mrs Tweedy snapped a collar around Ginger's neck – BLAM! Something feathery whizzed out of the air vent, knocking her and Dr Fry to the floor.

Molly ducked out of her hiding spot and raced to her mum's side. She set Ginger free but the collar had already done its work.

'I love it here!' said Ginger, giggling.

'Mum, no!' cried Molly. 'Dad?' she said, seeing a dazed Rocky on the floor.

Rocky looked up. Mrs Tweedy and Dr Fry were closing in. He had to get them away from Ginger and Molly. What could he do?

He began to dance. The Funky Chicken, the Robot, every move he knew! Once Molly and Ginger had escaped, Rocky ran for the lift, the doors closing just in time.

'FIND THOSE CHICKENS!' Mrs Tweedy screamed.

As Molly led Ginger along a corridor, Babs, Bunty and Mac came around the corner.

'Thank heavens you escaped from that horrible woman!' said Bunty. They had seen everything on the screens in reception.

'Mrs Tweedy is the best!' giggled Ginger. Bunty looked shocked.

'Raah!' An angry guard appeared. CLUNK! Two rats and a grate fell on his head.

'Uncle Nick! Uncle Fetcher!' cried Molly.

'Going up!' cried Ginger, jumping onto a machine of revolving buckets. Everyone jumped into the bucket after her. PING! They got Ginger's collar off just as all the buckets tipped over.

'WAAAH!' They all fell down, down, down . . . into a big corn silo.

'What happened?' asked Ginger, blinking. 'Where are we?'

'Mum, you're okay!' cried Molly in relief. Ginger hugged her daughter, then looked around. The only way out of the corn silo was through a hatch high above them. They were stuck.

'We need a miracle to get out of here,' said Bunty.

'Hey!' came a voice from the hatch above. It was Rocky!
'I'm coming down!' he shouted.

'No!' cried the chickens. He was their only way out!

Rocky jumped into the silo, then realised what he
had done. 'Sorry,' he said.

Molly began to cry. 'This is all my fault!'

'No, Molly,' said Rocky. 'It's my fault! I should have
thought before I jumped.'

'It's my fault!' said Ginger. 'I should have told you the truth about
the mainland, Molly. I always hated being fenced in – so why
should you be any different?' She looked at her daughter.

'I was afraid that you were too
much like me.'

'What's wrong with being like
you?' asked Molly.

'Nothing!' said Rocky.
'Because your mum
is the best! And she
always has a plan.'

But this time Ginger
had no plan. Things
looked hopeless.

A guard rushed into the control room. 'The runaway chickens are stuck in the corn silo!'

Mrs Tweedy smiled. 'Excellent,' she said, hitting a switch labelled **GRINDER**.

In the silo, the corn began to move. It was being sucked into the grinder – along with the chickens! Everyone panicked. Rocky looked at all the corn and had an idea.

'Popcorn!' he said. It was one of his favourite snacks on the island.

'Yes!' cried Ginger. 'But we need heat!'

'Will this work?' said Mac, getting a firework from her backpack.

'Perfect!' said Rocky, standing it upside down in the corn. Clever Molly used Mac's glasses to focus a beam of light onto the firework fuse. It lit. The rocket exploded, and the corn began to POP!

The gang shot out of the silo on a wave of popping corn. They landed on the roof, surprising Fowler. He had just set up a zip wire over the fence.

'Let's fly this crazy coop,' shouted Rocky.

Ginger hesitated. 'I'm going back,' she said.

'For Frizzle?' asked Molly.

'For Frizzle – and all the chickens,' said Ginger.

'Yes!' cried Molly. 'I'm coming, too!' Everyone cheered. They were in this together!

Rocky looked at Molly. 'Are you ready for this?' he asked.

'I was hatched ready, Dad!' said Molly, excitedly. Rocky smiled. She was just like her mum!

The rescue mission began. Ginger and Rocky broke back into Fun-Land Farms and hurried up to the control room, where they set up a trip wire for Dr Fry. He fell and got his head stuck in an egg sculpture.

Meanwhile the Sir Eat-A-Lot truck was waiting for its first nugget delivery and Mrs Tweedy was getting impatient. 'Why isn't the processor working, Dr Fry?' she shouted into her walkie-talkie.

She marched into the control room to find Dr Fry stumbling around, and Ginger and Rocky approaching three remote controls.

Rocky leapt and grabbed the nearest remote while Mrs Tweedy snatched another. Rocky's remote worked the coffee machine. Mrs Tweedy's remote switched on the collars! She pressed **ALL CHICKENS.**

'Let's make nuggets!' she snarled. Down below, every single chicken's collar flashed and they all flocked to the escalator excitedly.

At that moment Molly and the gang burst into Fun-Land.

'Frizzle!' shouted Molly. She and Mac pushed through the crowds and unpicked Frizzle's collar. Frizzle shook her head and then beamed. 'You came back for me!' she said.

'That's what friends do,' said Molly. 'Me and you, kidda – all the way!'

WHOOSH! Hundreds of chickens swept Frizzle, Molly and the gang onto the escalator, heading directly to the nugget processor!

Rocky realised the third remote control was the one that switched off the collars! He leapt at it. So did Mrs Tweedy. She knocked them both over the balcony. Rocky fell into some cables and the remote landed in a bucket.

Along came Ninja Ginger. She jumped off the balcony and ran for the remote.

'Go, Ginger!' cried Rocky.

But Mrs Tweedy was onto her – and now she had an axe! As Ginger grabbed at the remote, Mrs Tweedy switched on the bucket machine.

'No!' Ginger cried as the bucket carried the remote away. It tipped the remote out onto some wires, right above the processor.

Molly saw what was happening above and moved fast. Climbing onto Frizzle's shoulders, she leapt onto a passing bucket, which carried her up to where her parents were struggling to stop Mrs Tweedy. She jumped out and edged her way towards the remote.

'I've got this, Dad,' Molly shouted, grabbing the remote. 'Help Mum!'

Mrs Tweedy had Ginger trapped. Then she heard Molly.

'What have we here – a little you?' she snarled, snatching her up.

Molly threw the remote to Ginger. 'Press the button, Mum! NOW!' The chickens were almost in the processor!

Ginger didn't know what to do. If she turned off the collars, what would Mrs Tweedy do to Molly?

But Rocky was ready and waiting to swoop in. Ginger saw him and hit the button. The chickens were FREE! Rocky swung at Mrs Tweedy on a cable, knocking the axe out of her hand.

'OW!' Mrs Tweedy cried, as Molly bit her. She shook Molly off into the processor – but Ginger caught her just in time. Now they were both dangling over it, struggling to hold on!

'I got you!' shouted Rocky, grabbing onto his family. Mrs Tweedy marched over.

'You three might make a bucketful,' she snarled, about to kick them to their doom.

CLANG! The axe, which had been tangled up in a cable, swung across the gangway and knocked Mrs Tweedy into the processor instead!

Rocky swept Molly and Ginger into a tight hug, then cried, 'Let's go!'

BAM! All the chickens burst outside and flattened Mr Smith. Bunty led them into his truck. Rocky, Ginger and Molly raced out of the building and leapt into the front seat. With Nick and Fetcher working the pedals, they drove off at high speed.

Suddenly, a crumby hand came through the window and grabbed the wheel.

'AAH!' screamed the chickens. A nugget-shaped Mrs Tweedy was on the roof!

'Get her off!' shouted Ginger, trying to drive over the moat bridge.

WHIZZ! From nowhere, Fowler appeared on his zipline. He smashed into Mrs Tweedy, sending her into the moat. SPLASH! She was gone.

BOOM! Fun-Land Farm exploded. The nugget processor had over-heated.

It was all over. Time to go home.

Back on the island, the chickens were safe at last. Ginger, Rocky and the gang had saved every single chicken from Fun-Land Farms and now everyone was busy building extra hen houses and making new friends.

Rocky hugged Ginger. 'Looks like we finally got our happy ending,' he said.

'Let's call it our happy beginning,' said Ginger. She waved at Molly and Frizzle, who were floating above them in Fowler's cloud balloon.

Frizzle peered through her binoculars. 'Chicken Farm beyond the North field – thirty birds to a cage!'

'It's GO TIME!' cried Ginger. Everyone cheered. They were on a rescue mission. No chicken would ever be left behind – not while Ginger and the gang were around!

MOLLY

Curious, adventurous, headstrong and brave – just like her mum. Molly will never abandon a chicken in need.

FRIZZLE

Daft Frizzle is a bit naive about the world, but she is kind and always looks out for her best friend, Molly.

GINGER

The natural leader of the flock and an amazing mum to Molly, Ginger is the mastermind behind the flock's freedom-fighting missions!

MEET THE GANG

Ginger, Rocky and the gang are always ready for the next adventure – especially when it means saving chicken-kind from the **Dawn of the Nugget!**

ROCKY

A relaxed, fun dad to Molly, whose heart is always in the right place. He's more of a 'do-er' than a thinker.

FOWLER

BABS

BUNTY

MAC

The Getaway Guy, Wool Specialist, Muscles and Brains make an unlikely crew, but this gang doesn't shy away from any mission – no matter how impossible!

Part pick-pockets, part street vendors, this good-hearted pair love playing uncle to Molly.

FETCHER

NICK

Cruel Mrs Tweedy hates all chickens (especially Ginger). She's bent on revenge – with the help of her eccentric husband, Dr Fry.

DR FRY

MRS TWEEDY

First published 2023 by Macmillan Children's Books
an imprint of Pan Macmillan
The Smithson, 6 Briset Street, London EC1M 5NR
EU representative: Macmillan Publishers Ireland Limited 1st Floor, The Liffey Trust Centre
117–126 Sheriff Street Upper, Dublin 1, D01 YC43
Associated companies throughout the world.
www.panmacmillan.com

ISBN: 978-1-0350-2300-4

Written by Amanda Li
Based on the film *Chicken Run: Dawn of the Nugget*
Text and illustrations © and ™ Aardman Animations Ltd 2023
All rights reserved. *Chicken Run: Dawn of the Nugget* is the registered Trade Mark
of Aardman Animations Ltd.
Chicken Run: Dawn of the Nugget animated feature © Netflix 2023

1 3 5 7 9 8 6 4 2

A CIP catalogue record is available for this book from the British Library.

Printed in Spain

MIX
Paper | Supporting
responsible forestry
FSC® C116313
FSC
www.fsc.org